You Poop Here

PAUL MEISEL

HOLIDAY HOUSE ● NEW YORK

Ant poops on dirt.

And Beetle poops on dirt.

Monkey poops from a tree.

And Squirrel poops from a tree.

Grasshopper poops on a leaf.

And Bear poops on many leaves.

Elephant poops on grass.

Bat . . .

and Bee poop in air.

Alligator . . .

and Fish poop in water.

Seal poops on a rock.

And Gull poops on a rock.

Sheep . . .

and Llama poop on mountains.

Turtle . . .

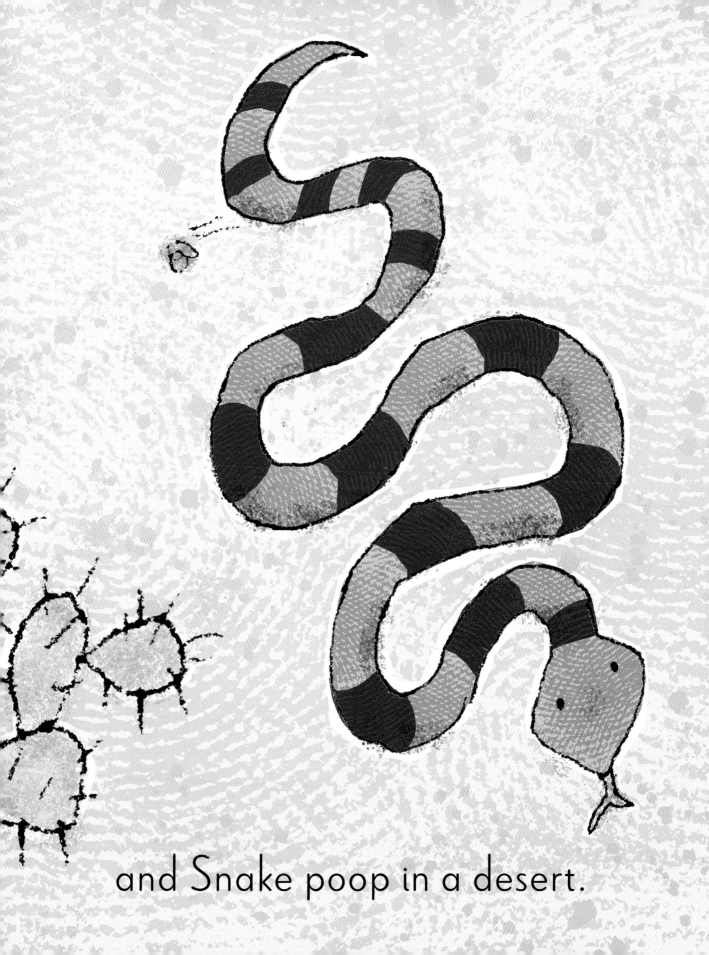

and Snake poop in a desert.

Jaguar . . .

and Sloth poop in a rainforest.

Where do you poop?

You poop here!

(And pee here too!)

WHAT IS POOP?

When you eat food, the food breaks down
into tiny, tiny parts.

Your body uses the food so you can stay alive.

But your body can't use all of the food.

The unused food becomes poop.

Pooping is very important.

It keeps your body clean and healthy.

FUN FACTS ABOUT POOP

Alligator poop is like bird poop. There's a white part and a brownish-green part.

Ants have special places in their nest for pooping in order to keep the nest clean.

Bats poop and pee while flying. If they're hanging upside down, they'll go upright for a few seconds so that they can poop.

Elephants can poop as much as three hundred pounds a day.

Sloths come down from their trees once a week to poop, usually in the same place.